Lion

Bobcat

Panther

Tiger

Puma

Jaguar

Cheetah

Persian cat

Dedicated to all the cats in my life

Eric Carle **Have you seen my cat?**

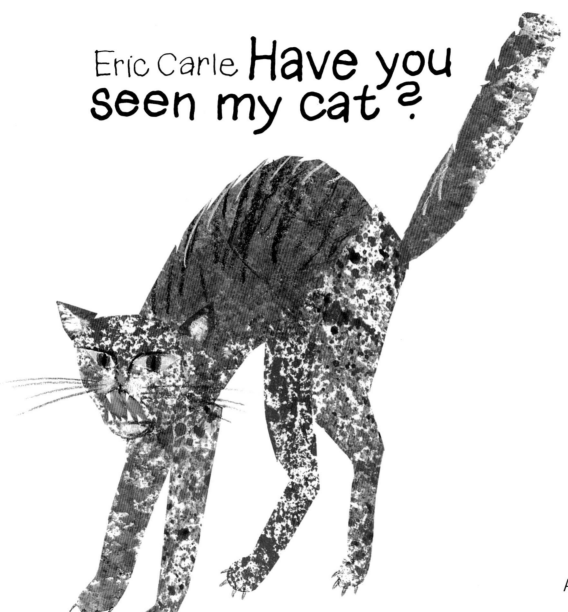

Aladdin Paperbacks

Have you seen my cat?

This is not <u>my</u> cat!

Have you seen my cat?

This is not <u>my</u> cat!

Have you seen
my cat?

This is not <u>my</u> cat!

Have you seen my cat?

This is not <u>my</u> cat!

Have you seen my cat?

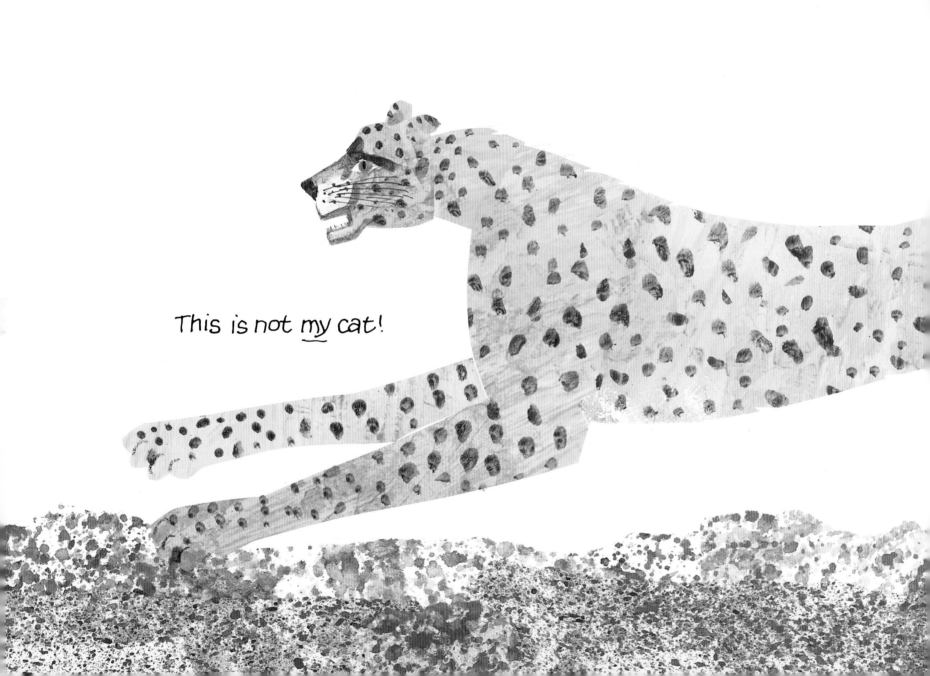

This is not <u>my</u> cat!

Have you seen my cat?

This is not <u>my</u> cat!

Have you seen my cat?

This is not <u>my</u> cat!

Where is my cat?

Have you seen my cat?

This is my cat!

First Aladdin Paperbacks edition September 1997
Copyright © 1987 by Eric Carle Corp.
Eric Carle's name and his signature logotype are
trademarks of Eric Carle.
Aladdin Paperbacks
An imprint of Simon & Schuster
Children's Publishing Division
1230 Avenue of the Americas
New York, NY 10020
Also available in a Simon & Schuster Books for Young Readers edition.
Manufactured in China
10 9 8 7 6 5 4 3 2 1
The Library of Congress has cataloged the hardcover edition as follows:
Carle, Eric.
Have you seen my cat?
Originally published: New York: F. Watts, 1973.
Summary: A young boy encounters all sorts of cats while searching for the one he
lost
(1. Cats—Fiction.  2. Picture books)  I. Title.
PZ7.C21476Hav    1987    [E]    87-15262
ISBN 0-689-87231-3

Lion

Bobcat

Panther

Tiger

Puma

Jaguar

Cheetah

Persian cat